MEET ALL THESE FRIENDS IN BUZZ BOOKS:

Thomas the Tank Engine
The Animals of Farthing Wood
James Bond Junior
Fireman Sam
Joshua Jones
Blinky Bill
Rupert
Babar

First published in Great Britain 1993 by Buzz Books,
an imprint of Reed Children's Books
Michelin House, 81 Fulham Road, London SW3 6RB
and Auckland, Melbourne, Singapore and Toronto

The Animals of Farthing Wood © copyright 1979 Colin Dann
Storylines © copyright EBU 1992
Text © copyright 1993 Reed International Books Limited
Illustrations © copyright 1993 Reed International Books Limited
Based on the novels by Colin Dann and the animation series
produced by Telemagination and La Fabrique for the BBC
and the European Broadcasting Union.
All rights reserved.

ISBN 1 85591 327 5

Printed in Italy by Olivotto

The Storm Shelter

Story by Colin Dann
Text by Mary Risk
Illustrations by The County Studio

The animals of Farthing Wood were on their way to White Deer Park, where humans couldn't destroy their homes. The route to safety now lay through the centre of town.

Weasel skipped along the pavement. "Weasels are wonderful..." she sang.

6

"Sssilence, Weasssel," Adder hissed.

There was a sudden rumble of thunder,
and a bolt of lightning struck the pavement
near Weasel. She danced about, howling.

"Ssserves you right," said Adder.

"A storm!" said Fox, looking up at the sky
in dismay. "That's all we need."

7

A minute later, it was pouring with rain.

"I can't stand thunder," said Father Rabbit, trembling. "It ruins my nerves. And I'll catch my death of a cold."

Before long the gutters were full of swiftly flowing water.

"What will we do?" cheeped the mice and voles. "We can't cross the road!"

Owl had flown up to a nearby church.

"You've found a nice dry place to shelter from the storm," said Whistler, landing in the belfry beside her.

Owl glared at him. "I'm just getting a bird's eye view," she said.

Whistler peered out at the others. "Those little ones need help!" he said, and he took off again.

"Help! Help!" called the frightened mice and voles, as they struggled to swim across the flooded gutters.

One at a time, Whistler fished the animals out of the water with his beak and dropped them safely onto the muddy church green.

In the gutter, the stream of water was carrying Adder straight towards a drain, when suddenly Whistler swooped down and caught her in his mouth.

"Thanksss," Adder hissed as Whistler set her down on the green.

Everyone was feeling wet and miserable.

"Follow me to the church!" Fox said.
"There's sure to be a porch round the
other side. We can shelter there."

11

But the old porch had fallen in.

"Now what will we do?" said Badger.

Mole tugged at Badger's fur. "Let me get down, Badger, please," he said.

"Oh, all right, Moley," said Badger, "but don't start digging, will you?"

Mole slid to the ground, and ran off.

"Where's he going?" barked Fox. "Come back here, Mole!"

A few minutes later, Mole was back.

"Badger!" he squeaked. "I've found a way into the church! Come and see!"

Everyone followed Mole round to a hole, low down in the church wall.

"Well done, Moley," panted Badger, as he squeezed his big, furry body through the narrow gap.

It was dark in the church, but at least it was dry. The animals nosed around to find comfortable places for themselves.

"We can rest now," said Fox. "Let's settle down and go to sleep."

A few minutes later, the only sounds were Badger's gentle snores.

The animals were so tired that they slept late the next morning. They didn't hear the workers clearing away the loose plaster from the gap in the wall. They didn't hear them fill it up with new stones, and cement over the cracks.

When they finally did wake up, it was too late.

"We're trapped!" Fox said. "We can't get out!"

15

"This is all your fault, Mole," said Father Rabbit meanly.

A tear rolled down Mole's fat cheek.

"It isn't anyone's fault," said Vixen. "We had to get out of the rain and Mole found us some shelter."

"Thank you, Vixen," gulped Mole.

Toad scratched at his dry skin. "Wouldn't it be wonderful to be beside the pond in White Deer Park right now?" he said.

"Tell us about White Deer Park, Toad," said Vixen.

"Yes, tell us, Toad," clamoured the other animals excitedly.

Only Toad had ever been to White Deer Park, and the other animals were curious to find out more about their future home.

"Is it a big place?" asked Badger.

"The forest is enormous, mateys," said Toad dreamily. "And there are lots of animals there. The Great White Stag is the leader at White Deer Park. He is very kind, and his coat shines in the dark..."

"Listen!" said Fox. "What's that noise?"

The doors opened and the church filled
with people dressed in their finest clothes.

"Run for it!" screamed Weasel.

"No!" said Fox. "Hide here, behind the
organ, and wait until they've gone."

The animals waited. Suddenly there was
a deafening, terrifying sound! The organist
had started playing.

18

The mice had hidden in the organ pipes,
but now a surge of air blew them right
out of the top of the organ!

They landed with a crash on the keys of
the organ. The surprised organist suddenly
found a pair of mice running up and down
under his fingers. As he tried to catch them,
the music became a jangled blare of sound.

Weasel was dancing about behind the organ. "Run! Run!" she squealed.

"Please, everyone. Keep still and wait," Badger growled. He clamped his great paw on top of Weasel to pin her down.

Mother Rabbit was quivering with fright.

"Don't panic!" she whimpered.

She was too late. Father Rabbit darted out of the hiding place, and lolloped down the aisle. Weasel wriggled free and scampered after him, followed by several of the smaller animals.

The people in the church panicked.

"Ugh! Help!" they shouted.

Some people tried to catch the animals, while others took fright.

"Hah! The humans are afraid!" chuckled Weasel. What fun she was having!

Then the doors swung open as the bride arrived at the church. The animals ran towards the open doors and freedom.

But Mole wasn't fast enough. A large hand caught him by the tail. Badger heard his squeaks. He bared his teeth and growled at the man, then gently took Mole in his paw and placed him safely on his back.

"Oh thank you, Badger," said Mole, snuggling into his friend's furry shoulder.

Weasel was enjoying herself. She ran round the feet of a frightened lady, teasing her.

Then suddenly, a shadow loomed overhead. Weasel looked up to see a man aiming to trap her beneath his top hat! She stopped laughing, and dashed out of the door.

Whistler's long legs clipped a lady's hat as he flew out of the church, whisking it off her head.

"Oo! Ow!" the lady shouted.

Owl was unlucky too. Her sharp claws got caught in the bride's veil. It floated off the bride's head and into the air.

24

The poor bride nearly fainted. Birds
flapped overhead, and a badger, a mole,
two foxes, a rabbit, a toad, a weasel and a
whole collection of squirrels, mice, voles
and shrews were milling about underfoot.

The bride threw up her hands in horror,
accidentally throwing her flowers too.

"Very nice!" said Weasel, catching the bouquet. She began to play with it.

"Weasel, come on!" said Fox.

Weasel tossed the flowers into the air, and the bride's eager hands caught them. She tried to catch her veil, too, but it sank to the ground.

Suddenly, something beneath the veil reared up, hissing. Adder wriggled free, and slithered out of the church.

"All'sss well that endsss well," she whispered, looking back through the church door.

The bride thought so too. She put on her veil, tidied her bouquet and marched up the aisle to her bridegroom. The organist, forgetting the mice, played an enthusiastic rendition of *Here Comes the Bride* !

The animals ran from the church, scattering in different directions.

The squirrels raced up a pole, chattering to each other. The rabbits panicked and fell into a ditch. Adder followed the smaller animals to a field of long grass.

Badger and Weasel raced away from the church, and ended up in the centre of town, where they found an open trap door. They dashed down the ramp and hid in the dark cellar.

Fox and Vixen were following Toad.

"White Deer Park is just across that field!" panted Toad. "Nearly there, mateys!"

"Slow down!" called Kestrel, from overhead. "Some of the animals are being left behind!"

"Oh no!" groaned Fox, looking back.

"They'll be okay," said Hare. "Let's go!"

"No," Fox said firmly. "We must find the others. After all we've been through on our journey, the animals of Farthing Wood will enter White Deer Park together. "